YOO-HOO, LADY BUG!

Mem Fox

illustrated by
Laura Ljungkvist

Beach Lane Books ▪ New York London Toronto Sydney New Delhi

For Linda Candy and her loved ones
—M. F.

This one's for you, Ebba!
—L. L.

BEACH LANE BOOKS
An imprint of Simon & Schuster Children's Publishing Division
1230 Avenue of the Americas, New York, New York 10020
Text copyright © 2013 by Mem Fox
Illustrations copyright © 2013 by Laura Ljungkvist
All rights reserved, including the right of reproduction in whole or in part in any form.
BEACH LANE BOOKS is a trademark of Simon & Schuster, Inc.
For information about special discounts for bulk purchases,
please contact Simon & Schuster Special Sales at 1-866-506-1949
or business@simonandschuster.com.
The Simon & Schuster Speakers Bureau can bring authors to your live event.
For more information or to book an event, contact the Simon & Schuster Speakers Bureau
at 1-866-248-3049 or visit our website at www.simonspeakers.com.
Book design by Lauren Rille
The text for this book is set in Lubalin.
The illustrations for this book are rendered digitally.
Manufactured in China
0213 SCP
First Edition
10 9 8 7 6 5 4 3 2 1
Library of Congress Cataloging-in-Publication Data
Fox, Mem, 1946–
Yoo-hoo, Ladybug! / Mem Fox ; illustrated by Laura Ljungkvist.—1st ed.
p. cm.
Summary: Invites the reader to search for Ladybug, who loves to hide.
ISBN 978-1-4424-3400-4 (hardcover)
ISBN 978-1-4424-3401-1 (eBook)
[1. Stories in rhyme. 2. Ladybugs—Fiction.] I. Ljungkvist, Laura, ill. II. Title.
PZ8.3.F8245Yoo 2013
[E]—dc23
2012009047

Ladybug *loves* to hide.

Yoo-hoo, Ladybug!

Where are you?

There you are . . .

afloat in the bath
with Duck and Giraffe!

Yoo-hoo,
Ladybug!
Where are you?

There you are . . .

tucked in a box
with Rabbit and Fox!

Yoo-hoo,
Ladybug!
Where are you?

There you are . . .

stuck on the stairs
with a couple of bears!

Yoo-hoo,

Ladybug!

Where are you?

There you are . . .

outside the house
with Chicken and Mouse!

Yoo-hoo,

Ladybug!

Where are you?

There you are . . .

up in the tree
with Bluebird and Bee!

Yoo-hoo,

Ladybug!

Where are you?

Ladybug?
Have you flown away?

Is our game over
for the rest of the day?

Where are you, Ladybug?

There you are!

Zooming around . . .

in your very own car!